# Hotel 1 2 3

## This book is dedicated
## to the two "M"s.
## DW

First published by David & Charles Children's Books in 2000.
This edition published under license from
David & Charles Children's Books.
First published in the United States by Holiday House in 2000.

Printed and bound in Belgium
Library of Congress Cataloging-in-Publication Data
Wojtowycz, David.
Animal antics from 1 to 10 / David Wojtowycz.
p. cm.
Summary: A counting book in which zany animal characters engage in
improbable activites in an unusual hotel.
ISBN 0-8234-1552-X (hardcover)
1. Counting—Juvenile literature. 2. Animals—Juvenile literature. [1. Counting.
2. Animals.] I. Title: Animal antics from 1 to 10. II. Title.
QA113.W64 2000
513.2'11—dc21

99-044460

# Animal Antics
David Wojtowycz

## from 1 to 10

Elevators

Rooms 1–10

Holiday House / New York

# 1

## one
## warthog
## wearing
## a wig

# 2

two
tangoing
toucans

# 3
## three
### thirsty
### flamingos

# 4

## four
## frightened
## frogs

# 5

## five
## feasting
## foxes

# 6

## six
## sleep-
## walking
## skunks

# 7

## seven
## singing
## sheep

# eight
## energetic
## eagles

# 9

## nine
## polite
## pigs

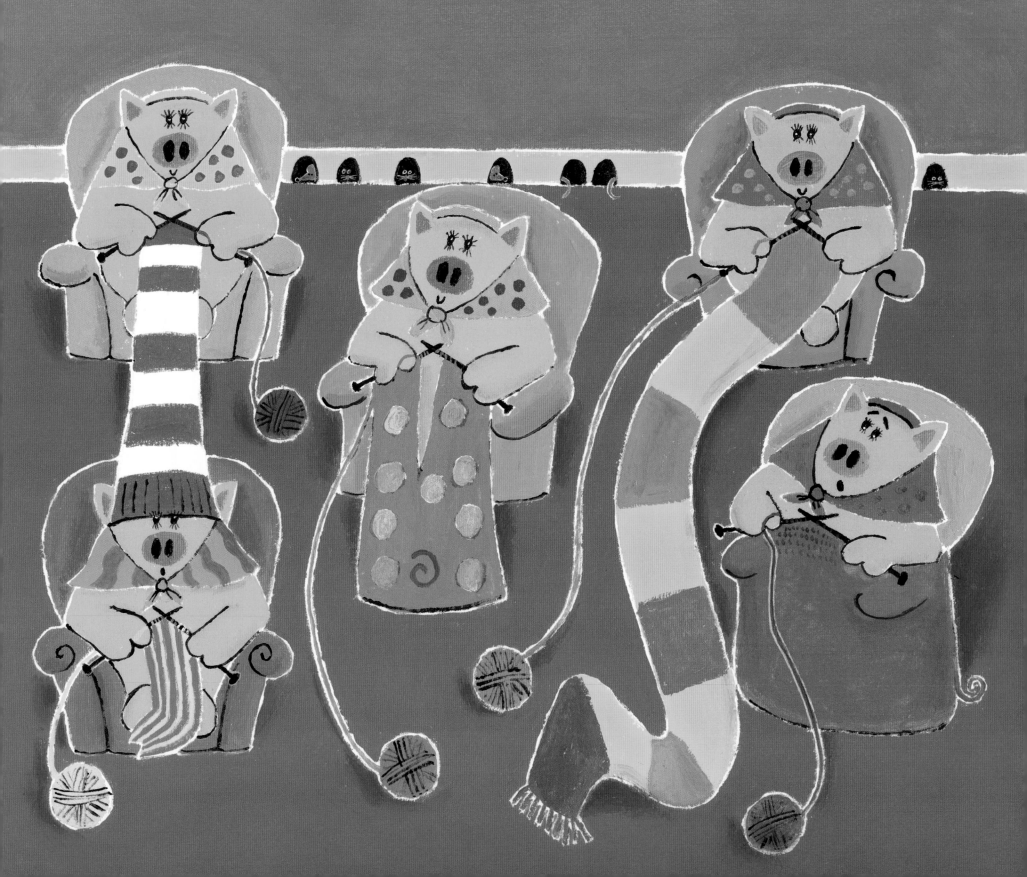

# 10

## ten
## tigers
## in tutus

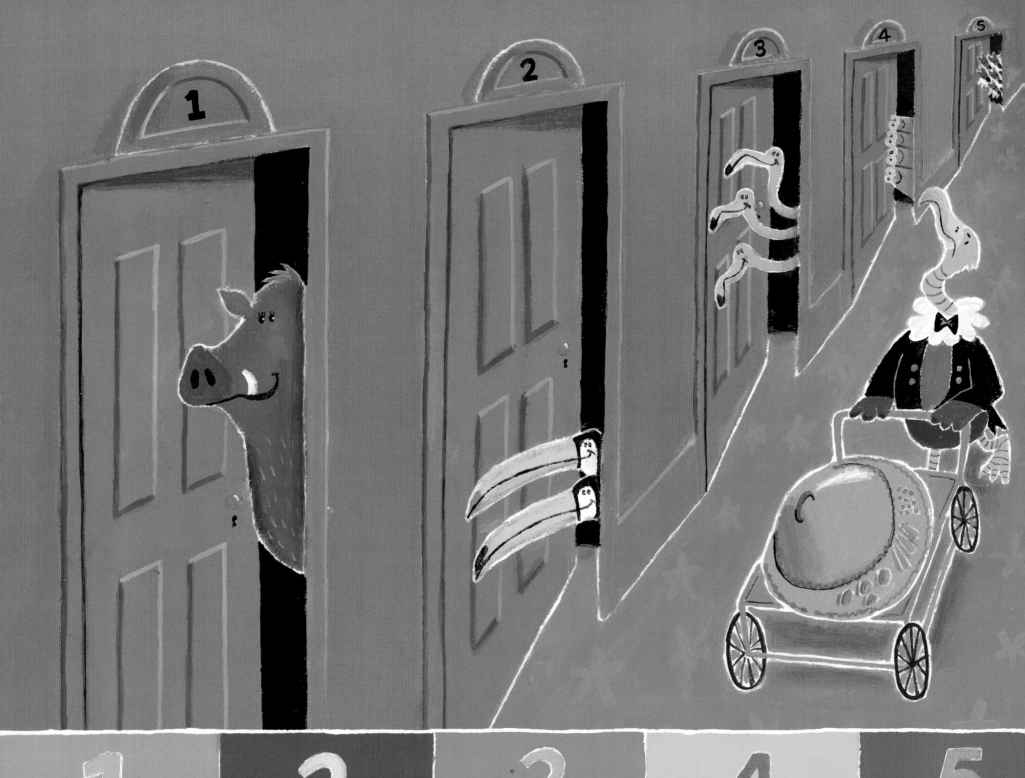

1 one    2 two    3 three    4 four    5 five

6 six 7 seven 8 eight 9 nine 10 ten